SOLOS FOR JAZZ TENOR SAX

CLASSIC JAZZ SOLOS

AS PLAYED BY:

JOHN COLTRANE

STAN GETZ

COLEMAN HAWKINS

OLIVER NELSON

SONNY ROLLINS

ANALYSES AND

NOTE-FOR-NOTE

TRANSCRIPTIONS BY

STUART ISACOFF

COMPLETE WITH

A CATALOG OF

JAZZ PHRASES BY

EACH ARTIST

CARL FISCHER, inc.
62 Cooper Square New York, NY 10003

Copyright © 1985 by Carl Fischer, Inc., New York
62 Cooper Square, New York, NY 10003
International Copyright Secured.
All rights reserved including
public performance for profit.
Printed in the U.S.A.

ATJ302   ISBN 0-8258-0381-0

CONTENTS

	Introduction **5**
	Elements of Style **7**
COLEMAN HAWKINS	Body and Soul **8**
SONNY ROLLINS	Dig **12**
JOHN COLTRANE	Epistrophy **16**
	Good Bait **19**
STAN GETZ	Desafinado **30**
JOHN COLTRANE	Stella by Starlight **33**
	Round Midnight **36**
OLIVER NELSON	Stolen Moments **40**
JOHN COLTRANE	Giant Steps **43**
	Catalogue of Phrases on V-I and II-V-I Progressions **50**
	Discography **55**

INTRODUCTION

Jazz was invented in 1902 by Jelly Roll Morton. Or so Morton claimed to the editors of Ripley's *Believe It Or Not*. They believed it.

Ever since, this music has found itself at the center of controversy. The great pianist Ignacy Paderewski called it "a terrible revenge by the culture of the Negroes on that of the whites." In the 1920s, the editor of *The Etude* linked jazz to America's crime rate. Russia's Maxim Gorky described it in terms of "wild screaming, hissing, rattling, wailing, moaning, cackling." "Bestial cries are heard," he wrote "Neighing horses, the squeal of a brass pig, crying jackasses, amorous quacks of a monstrous toad . . . " John Philip Sousa charged that "some of it makes you want to bite your grandmother."

Yet, since the turn of the century, "serious" composers have been delighting in the sound of jazz and writing pieces that celebrate its complex rhythms and colorful harmonies. Debussy and Stravinsky each produced several ragtimes. Milhaud, in *La Creation du monde*, gave us a classical dixieland work. Ravel was deeply influenced by George Gershwin, and Aaron Copland composed a *Jazz Concerto* and *Four Piano Blues*. Today's jazz has merged remarkably with contemporary classical traditions, not only in its impressionist harmonies and extended chromaticism, but in expressionist and even serial techniques as well.

Actually, there has been a partnership of sorts all along. One of the most important features of jazz is its reliance on improvisation, and this was once a common element in the classical tradition. "Whenever I play this concerto," said Mozart, referring to his *Piano Concerto* in D Major (K. 175), "I play whatever occurs to me at the moment." One of Mozart's contemporaries reported that his improvised performances were truly extraordinary. "If I dared to pray to the Almighty to grant me one more earthly joy," he wrote, "it would be that I might once again hear Mozart improvise."

Before Mozart's time, Baroque masters were equally adept at thrilling audiences with spontaneous variation and embellishment on fixed themes. Musicians were expected, as a matter of course, to be able to invent countermelodies and to improvise whole sections of works. However, improvisatory artists had their critics in those times, as well. The historical record contains, for example, a colorful outburst let loose by composer Josquin des Prez upon hearing a singer ornament one of his pieces beyond recognition. "You ass," he exclaimed, "if I had wanted that many notes I would have written them in." In fact, both J.S. Bach and Mozart wrote ornaments into their works so that others would hesitate to change the written versions.

Nevertheless, Bach did not hesitate to change a melody composed by Vivaldi, as the example below demonstrates:

Many jazz musicians make use of melodic ornamentation in a way which reflects this tradition at its roots in the sixteenth century. Charts containing examples of ways to ornament an interval fill several manuals of Renaissance music instruction. Adding notes in this manner to a given interval is not all that different from the approach taken by, say, Miles Davis in ornamenting the intervals contained in the chord tones of a given harmony.

Increased chromaticism and rhythmic complexity make jazz improvisations seem quite different from these earlier examples, but the basic principles of spontaneous composition used bear many similarities. There is less mystery to this art than many believe — and more art than critics have charged.

The solos contained in this volume demonstrate many stylistic approaches to improvisation within set harmonic progressions. Comparisons of the techniques used by each of the artists represented will add a new dimension to the catalogue offered by our sixteenth century predecessors. To that end, a section at the back of this book compares "lines" each artist played over a simple V-I or II-V-I progression.

Of course the real art in these solos transcends such clinical analyses, but the opportunity to study the actual notes up close can be invaluable to an aspiring performer. And the discussions of each solo should help in clarifying the processes at work.

ELEMENTS OF STYLE

In the history of jazz style, players have been labeled "horizontal" (concerned with melodic development) or "vertical" (concerned with vertical harmonies), "hot" or "cool," and "inside" (tonal), "outside" (nontonal) or "modal." Like all labels, these can be helpful at times but most often obscure the true picture. The individual stamp of any important musician results from a combination of many diverse elements — a musical recipe shaped by the taste of the performer — which includes various approaches to harmonic motion, phrase length, instrumental range, rhythm, cadence, embellishment and tone.

In analyzing the work of John Coltrane in the context of solos by influential colleagues, certain *common* elements emerge which thread the history of jazz sax, and in effect define the art of contemporary improvisation. If Coleman Hawkins, for example, sticks closely to the harmonic rhythm of a tune but makes use of disjunct, angular motion, Sonny Rollins might in effect alter the harmonic rhythm through chromatic embellishments which "smooth" out the movement of *his* improvised line. John Coltrane will at times extend patterns of non-chord tones beyond Rollins' voice-leading filigree into a new world of harmonic color; at other times, he will work within a more static harmony, making use of that earlier style of Hawkins.

Making music always involves a conciliation between opposing elements. Even when arpeggiating chords, most soloists remain deeply concerned with melodic contour and the shaping of coherent musical phrases. (Coltrane's shocking departure from this *verité* will be examined later in his solo on *Giant Steps*.) Therefore the following notes on each of the transcriptions in this volume attempt to avoid sweeping generalities, and focus instead on the musical building blocks which go into the making of every musical work. Despite all differences, each artist defines his expressive language through the manipulation of the same raw materials, and most often with an awareness of a shared tradition.

Coleman Hawkins
BODY AND SOUL

Coleman Hawkins, known as "Bean," was born in Missouri in 1904, and served as a transitional force from "swing" to "bebop." Hawkins was noted for his attention to the harmonic structure of a tune, and developed his solos with a good deal of "vertical" material (arpeggiated harmonies). His melodic flair, however, was unfailing, as can be seen in his classic 1939 solo on "Body and Soul."

The "swing" elements of Hawkins' style are reflected in the regular harmonic motion and steady rhythmic pulse which underlie his improvisations, as well as in the thick, vibrating tone he produced. His flow of notes is non-stop, but the rhythmic variety within that flow creates a jagged feeling very different from the smooth eighth-note approach of the beboppers. The downbeat of almost every measure is strongly reinforced, making for short, clearly defined phrases within the overall kinetic rhythm.

Hawkins sticks very strictly to the harmonies of a tune, and emphasizes the changes both rhythmically and melodically:

His selection of pitches often involves arpeggiated harmonies, although this will vary. In the example below, arpeggiated phrases alternate with phrases in which the chord tones are ornamented by non-chord tones to create weaving melodic lines:

This "weaving" device is close to the bebop style of improvisation; Hawkins also uses chromatics as a colorful ornament:

His phrases are often organized through variation of a melodic germ:

This device occasionally leads to wide skips, which increase the feeling of verticalness:

Body and Soul
Words by Edward Heyman, Robert Sour and Frank Eyton. Music by John Green.

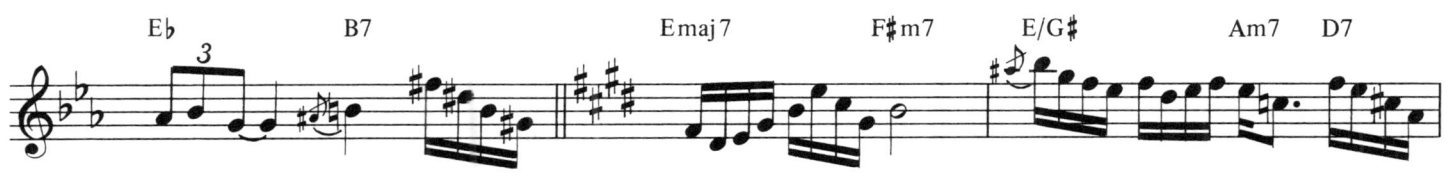

Sonny Rollins
DIG

Theodore "Sonny" Rollins was born in New York City in 1930, and has recorded with Miles Davis, Charlie Parker, Thelonious Monk, Max Roach, Clifford Brown and a host of other important musicians. Rollins is notorious for the self-imposed "retirements" which have interrupted a significant career, but he has always returned a stronger player after each absence.

"Dig" was recorded with Miles Davis in 1951. It is characteristic of the bebop style: long, weaving lines over dominant harmonies, familiar cadential patterns, the extensive use of eighth notes and occasional triplets.

The creation of the improvised line comes about through the interjection of pitches above and below the intervals of a tune's chords.

Sometimes the chords involved are "substitutes" for the originals: they may be a tritone away, or, as in the case below, a II chord may be substituted for a V chord. Notice the use of simple arpeggiation here for contrast.

Note also the use of the intervals of a tritone and perfect fourth as melodic cadences:

Even though the eighth note pattern is a significant feature of this style, Rollins is capable of creative rhythmic twists and a sense of musical coherence which elevates his playing to a high art.

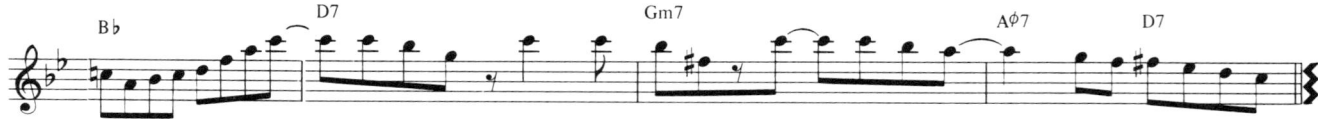

Dig
Miles Davis

John Coltrane
EPISTROPHY

John Coltrane has had perhaps the greatest influence on the development of contemporary saxophone style in the last thirty years. Born in 1926 in Hamlet, North Carolina, Trane performed with Dizzy Gillespie, Charlie Parker, Miles Davis and Thelonious Monk before founding one of the legendary bands of jazz history. Throughout his forty-one year life, he kept evolving, experimenting, and challenging musical conventions, yet there are strong ties in his music to the traditions which came before.

One element which pervades his approach to improvisation is an interest in playing the harmonies of a tune — not just in incorporating them into his melodic line, but in actually outlining them fully, regardless of how fast they are moving. When composing or practicing, Trane once said, he sat at the piano and ran through chord progressions and sequences. "After I've worked it out on the piano," he reported, "I then develop the song further on tenor, trying to extend it harmonically."

He once remarked that when he was playing with Miles Davis he didn't have anything to think about but "chords! chords! chords!" "I ended up playing them on my horn!" This caused some critics to urge Miles to get rid of Trane; in time, they all changed their tune.

"Epistrophy" was recorded with Thelonious Monk in 1957. It displays a good deal of rhythmic freedom in comparison to earlier players. It is clear, though, that Coltrane is sticking very closely to the harmonies of Monk's tune.

In both the tendency to arpeggiate, and the consequent leaps in range, Coltrane bears some similarity to the Hawkins school.

His experimentation with harmony and rhythm, and lack of interest in traditional melodic development, however, signal a new way.

Epistrophy
John Coltrane

John Coltrane
GOOD BAIT

"Good Bait," recorded in 1958, displays another side of Coltrane's art, the influence of the scaler, bebop-like approach associated with the Rollins camp. A virtuosic rhythmic variety shines through, however. Melodic coherence is achieved through both the variation technique within phrases and in repeated references to particular pitches or rhythms:

Trane makes use of the bebop device of substituting a II-V progression, or the VII chord against the original harmony.

And he has begun to develop a very personal catalogue of cadential phrases, which help identify his "sound."

Good Bait
Todd Damerson and Count Basie.

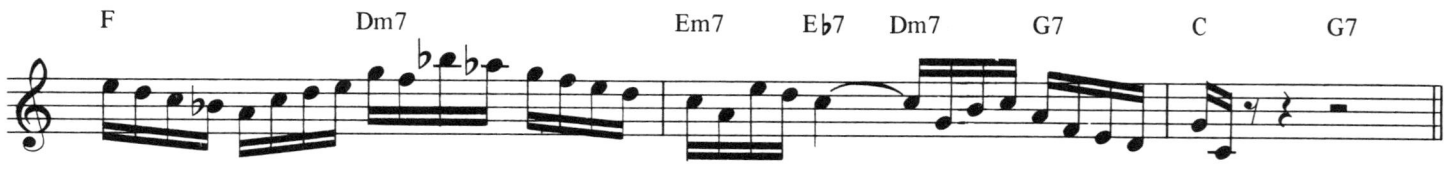

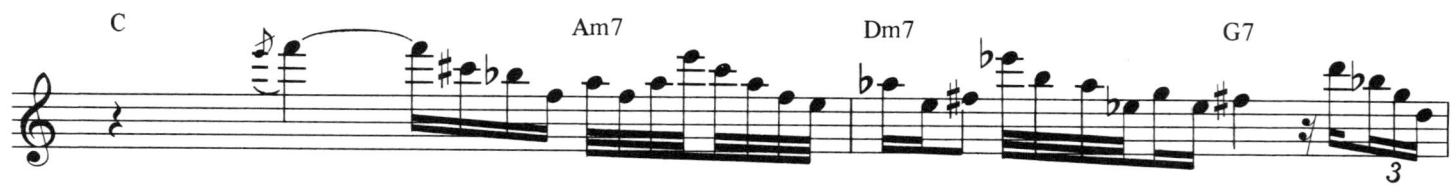

Copyright © 1944 (Renewed) by WB Music Corp. All Rights Reserved. Used by Permission.

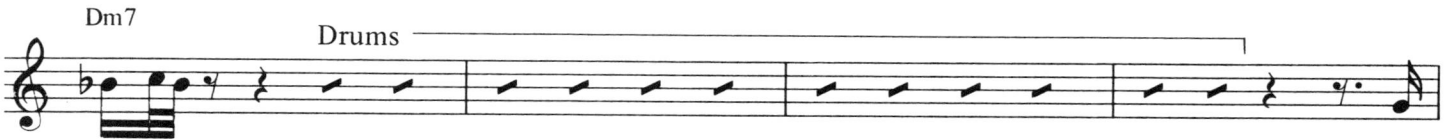

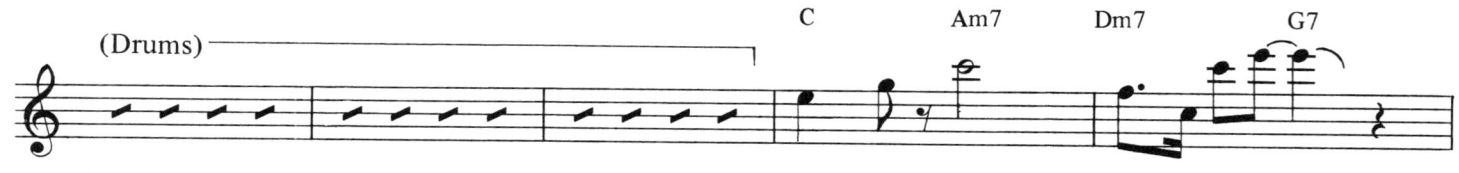

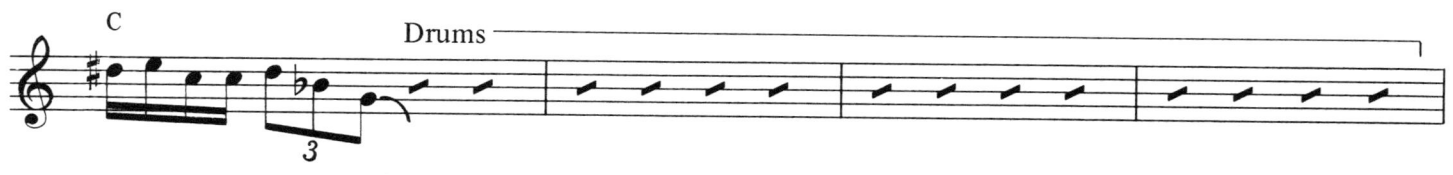

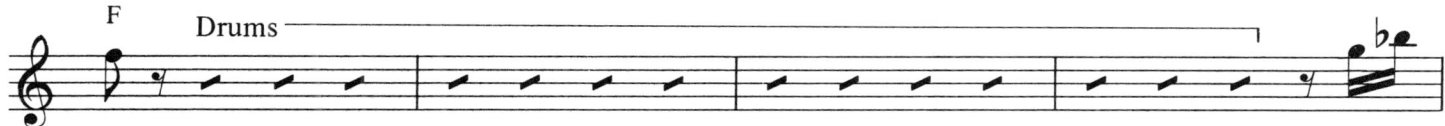

Stan Getz
DESAFINADO

Stan Getz continues to be one of the most elegant saxophone players of all time. Born in New York City in 1927, Getz performed with Jack Teagarden, Stan Kenton, Jimmy Dorsey, Benny Goodman and many others. Along with Zoot Sims, Herbie Steward and Serge Chaloff, he was one of the "Four Brothers" responsible for some of the greatest sounds produced by the Woody Herman band.

His light, airy sound and lyrical approach are perfectly suited to the South American music he turned to beginning in 1963, with the recording "Jazz Samba" — a collaboration with guitarist Charlie Byrd. Getz's solo on "Desafinado" exemplifies the "cool," melodic approach for which he is noted.

Note the melodic embellishment of the original melody.

Even when sticking closely to the harmonies through a kind of arpeggiation, Getz creates a relaxed, sweeping lyricism, sometimes making use of long, sustained tones to suspend the rhythmic flow.

Desafinado
Words by Newton Mendonca. Music by Antonio Carlos Jobim.

John Coltrane
STELLA BY STARLIGHT

Coltrane's approach to softer, lyrical works also contains elements of melodic embellishment. However, there are many more notes per measure than are evident in solos by Getz and other performers of the "cool" school and there is a reliance on harmonic arpeggiation.

"Stella By Starlight" was recorded with Miles Davis in 1958. Notice the technique of ornamenting the original melody.

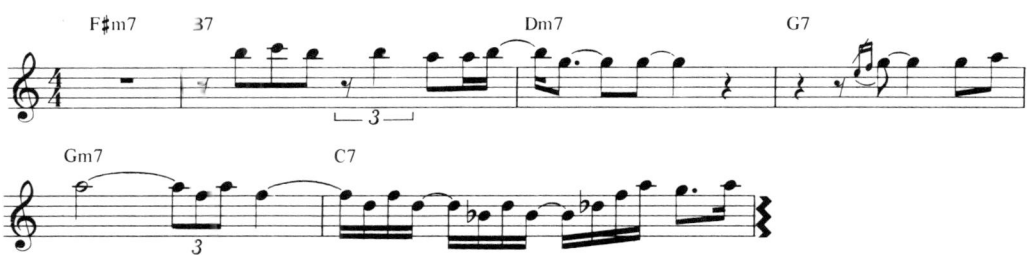

Once again, Coltrane's focus is on particular harmonies, or on particular pitches, which lends a "vertical" quality to the solo.

But Trane neatly ties up his phrases with additional very individual cadential formulas.

Stella by Starlight
Words by Ned Washington. Music by Victor Young.

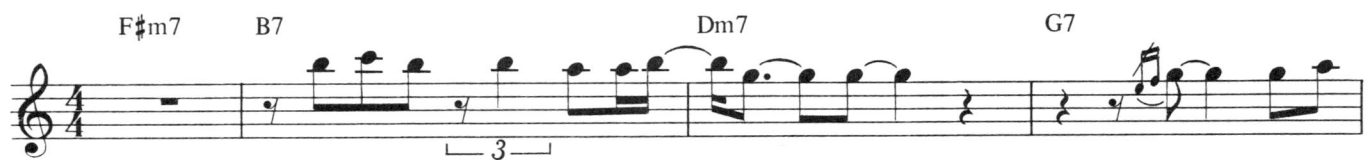

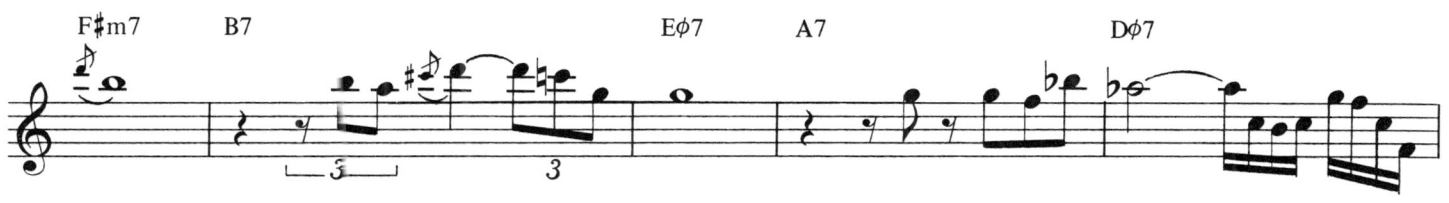

John Coltrane
ROUND MIDNIGHT

This Monk tune was recorded with Miles Davis in 1956, and features more of the ornamental approach. The tune is chromatically embellished right from the beginning.

Cadential phrases are interspersed between sections of the ornamented melody.

Harmonic arpeggiation and skips also appear.

And Coltrane's concern with harmonic color becomes reflected in his choice of ornamenting tones: rather than choosing simple scale or chromatic pitches, patterns begin to emerge which emphasize specific intervals and modal shadings. In the following examples, note the *whole tone*, and *half step-whole step* basis of the lines:

Round Midnight
Words by Bernie Hanighen. Music by Cootie Williams and Thelonious Monk

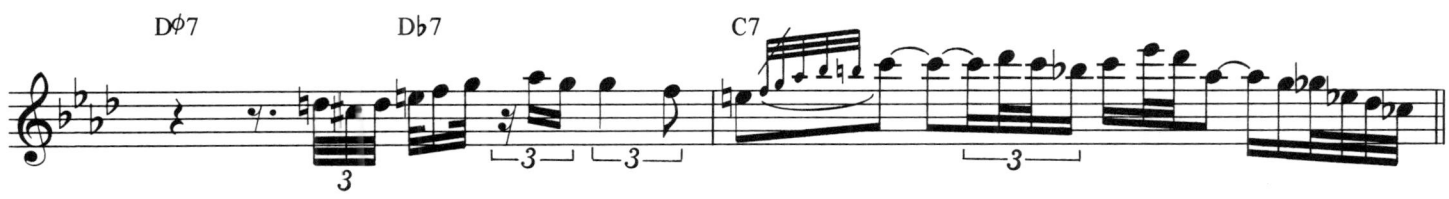

Copyright © 1944 by Warner Bros. Inc. Copyright Renewed. All Rights Reserved.

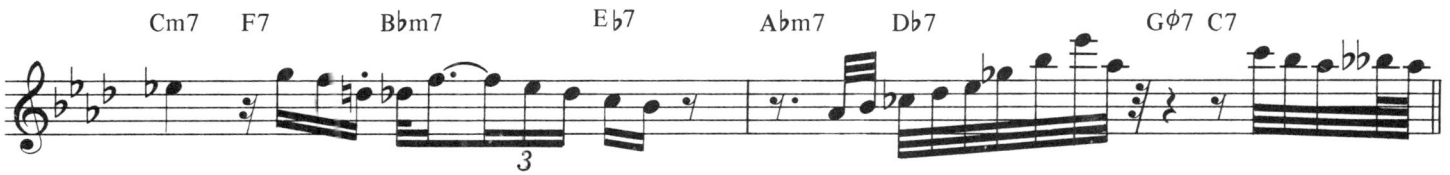

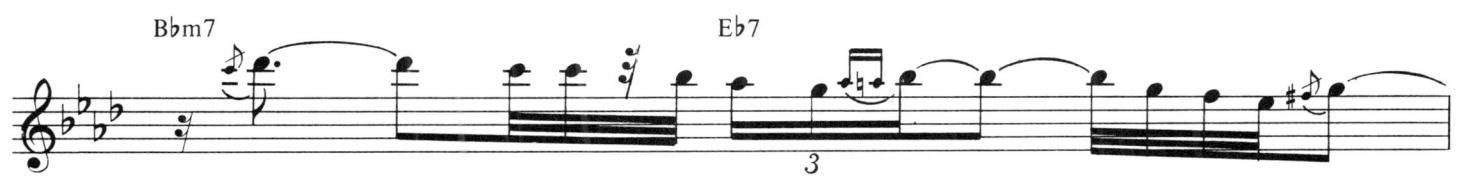

Oliver Nelson
STOLEN MOMENTS

Coltrane's interest in the tonal or modal coloring of phrases was further increased as a result of his study of Nicolas Slonimsky's *Thesaurus of Scales and Melodic Patterns* (Scribner & Sons). Slonimsky carved up the octave into various equal proportions, and constructed numerous melodic patterns which have since served many a jazz player.

Oliver Nelson, saxophonist, arranger and composer, put together a volume of his own melodic patterns, which served as a basis for much of *his* solo work. Nelson performed with Erskine Hawkins, Quincy Jones, Count Basie and Duke Ellington, and won *Downbeat's* reader poll for best arranger in 1967 and 1968.

Nelson was greatly influenced by Trane, and the solo on "Stolen Moments" is a classic example of Nelson's rich melodic sense placed within a format which exploits the pattern-making process mentioned above.

The opening sets the mood for the entire solo, with its quartal flavor:

Late period work by Coltrane often made use of similarly short, modal phrases tossed and turned in various permutations. An early example of this can be seen in these excerpts from Coltrane's solo on "Round Midnight." Note the way the phrases center around a particular repeating pitch.

This technique reaches its height for Coltrane in works like "A Love Supreme," where a sample phrase might appear as in the following example.

Nelson follows this repeating motif approach, but with the cool and facile elegance demonstrated by the softer work of Getz:

Finally, Nelson, like Coltrane, was interested in superimposing harmonic patterns over simple chord changes. Below, a pattern is created by building major triads on each of the three pitches of an E♭ augmented chord (a form of the ♭II of Dm). (By using these pitches the octave has been divided into three equal parts.) Nelson uses the ensuing harmonic progression B-G-E♭, to lead into the original Dm.

Stolen Moments
Oliver Nelson

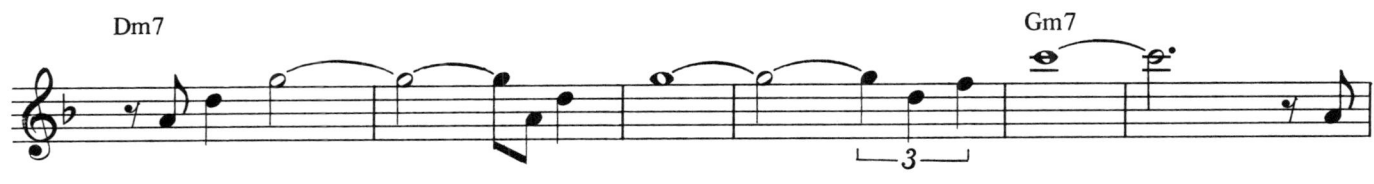

John Coltrane
GIANT STEPS

Coltrane once referred to his tendency to insert more and more harmonies into a piece of music by explaining, "I feel like I can't hear but so much in the ordinary chords we usually have going in the accompaniment. I just have to have more of a blueprint. It may be that sometimes I've been trying to force all those extra progressions into a structure where they don't fit."

One of the most heralded and startling developments in contemporary jazz occurred with the release of the album "Giant Steps." Here, Trane had let go of the rhythmic complexities of earlier solos, and seemed content to merely arpeggiate the series of chords underlying the tune. Of course, the tempo was so fast that hardly anyone noticed the lack of melodic craft.

There is an occasional turn or cadence to break the monotony:

For the most part, though, "Giant Steps" marks a radical departure from anything that had come before. This approach proved too stilted, and Trane eventually moved on to more advanced techniques. It remains, however, an interesting example of the "vertical" improvisation process taken to an extreme.

Giant Steps
John Coltrane

CATALOGUE OF PHRASES
ON V-I AND II-V-I PROGRESSIONS

1

2

3

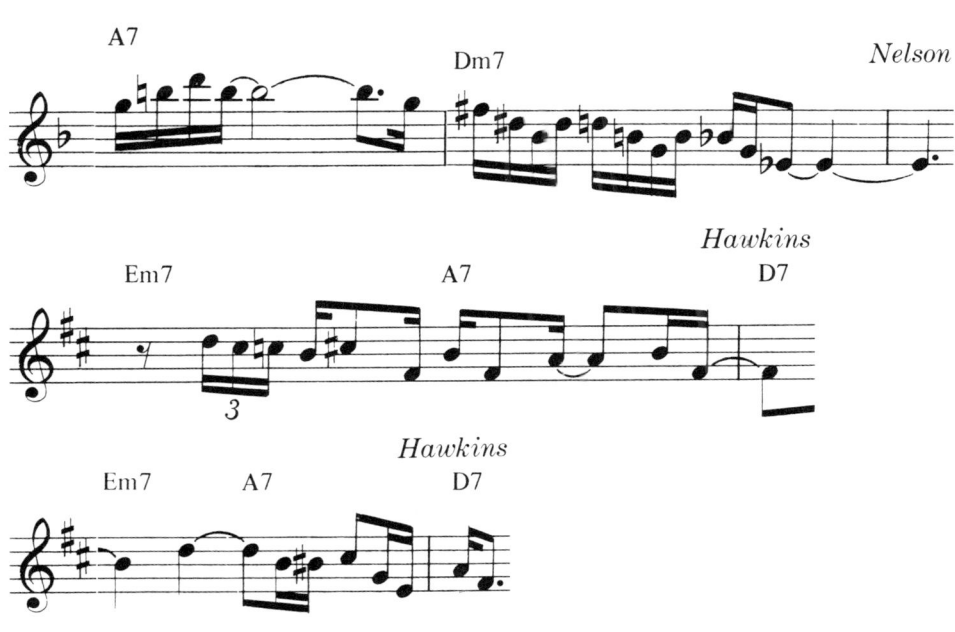

4

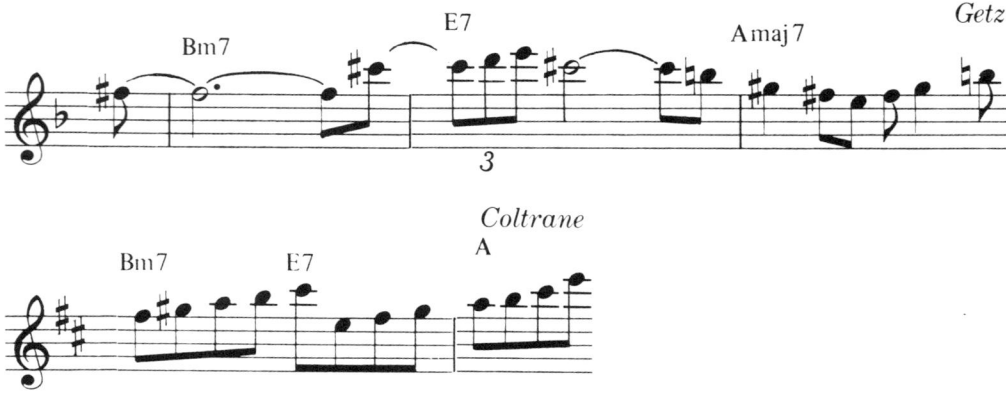

5

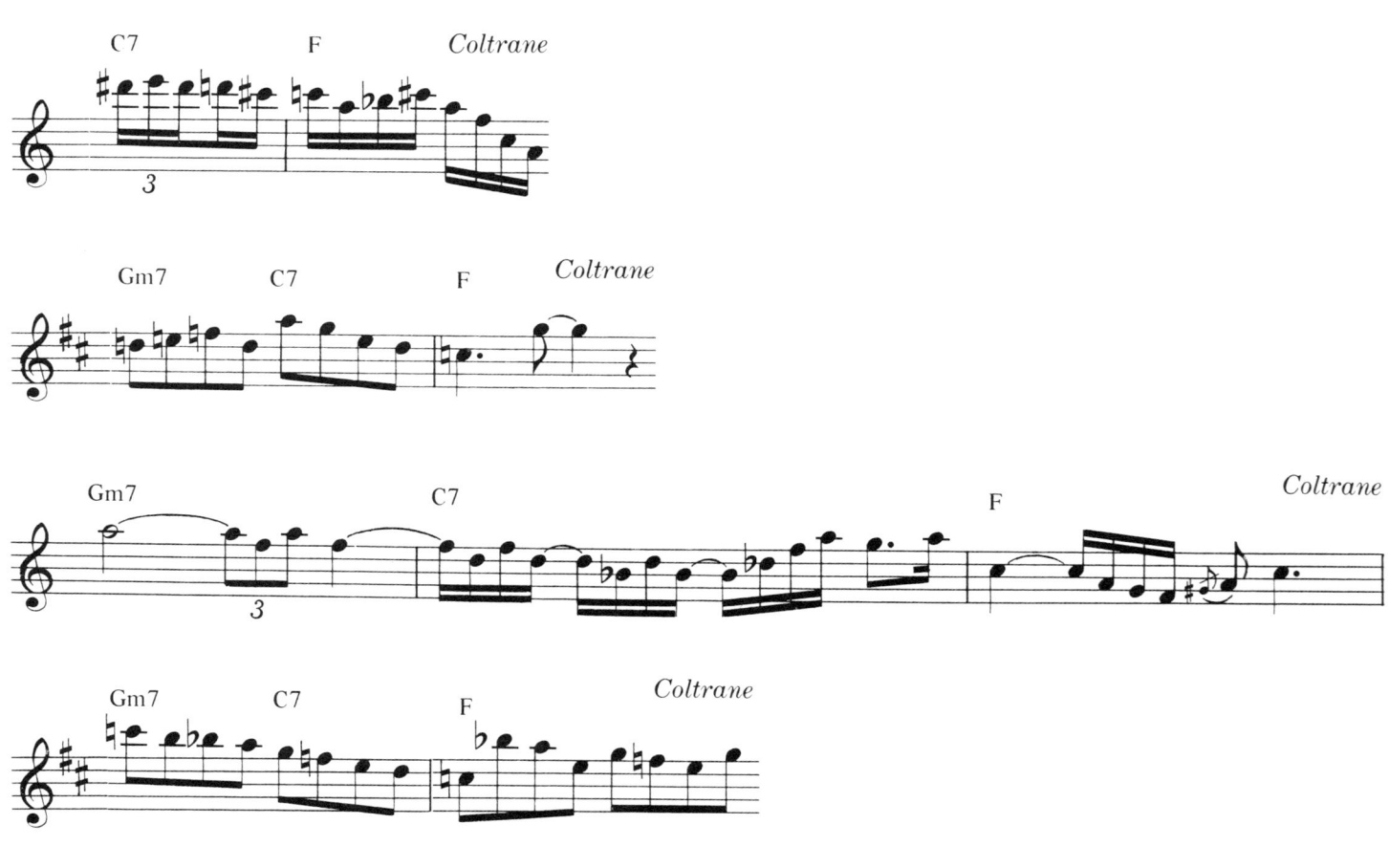

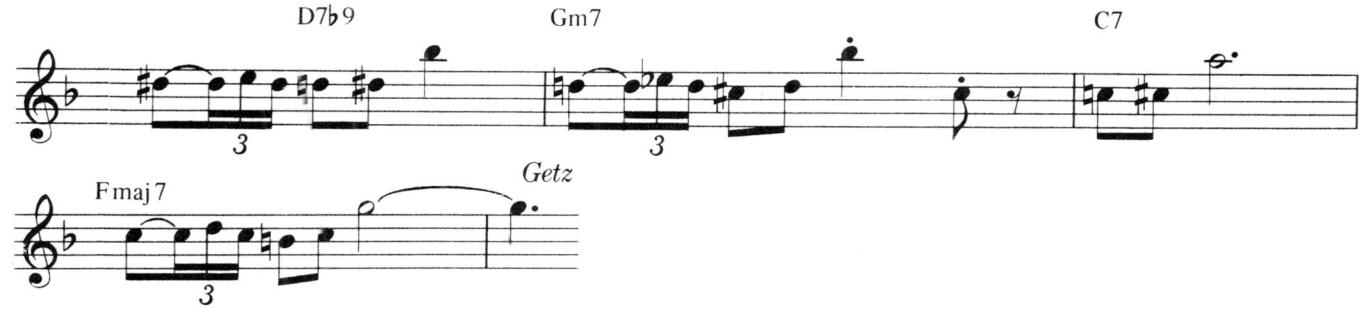

6

continued on the next page.

7

8

DISCOGRAPHY

COLEMAN HAWKINS	Body and Soul	"The Complete Coleman Hawkins" *RCA FXM1 7325*
SONNY ROLLINS	Dig	"Miles Davis featuring Sonny Rollins DIG" *Prestige 7012*
STAN GETZ	Desafinado	"Getz/Gilberto" *Verve UCV2099*
OLIVER NELSON	Stolen Moments	"The Blues and the Abstract Truth" *MCA C-29063*
JOHN COLTRANE	Stella By Starlight	"Basic Miles" *Columbia PC 32025*
	Epistrophy	"Thelonius Monk with John Coltrane" *Jazzland JLP 46*
	Good Bait	"Soultrane" *Prestige 7142*
	Giant Steps	"Giant Steps" *Atlantic SD-1311*
	Round Midnight	"Basic Miles" *Columbia PC 32025*